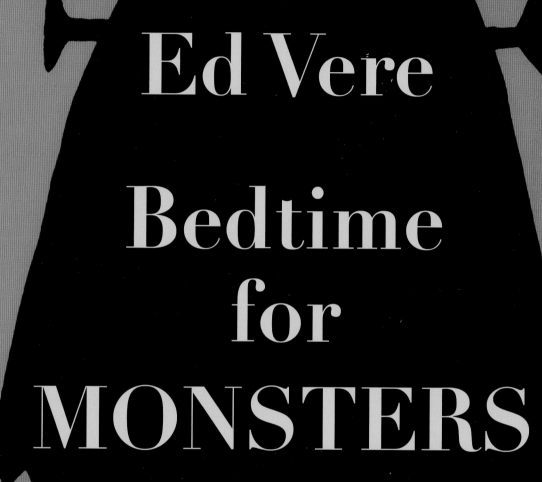

Ed Vere

Bedtime for MONSTERS

PUFFIN BOOKS

Published by the Penguin Group: London, New York, Australia, Canada, India, Ireland, New Zealand and South Africa
Penguin Books Ltd, Registered Offices: 80 Strand, London WC2R 0RL, England puffinbooks.com
First published 2011 Text and illustrations copyright © Ed Vere, 2011 edvere.com
Made and printed in China ISBN: 978–0–141–50239–7 001 – 10 9 8 7 6 5 4 3 2 1

PUFFIN

For
Rufus and Phoebe
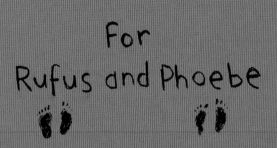

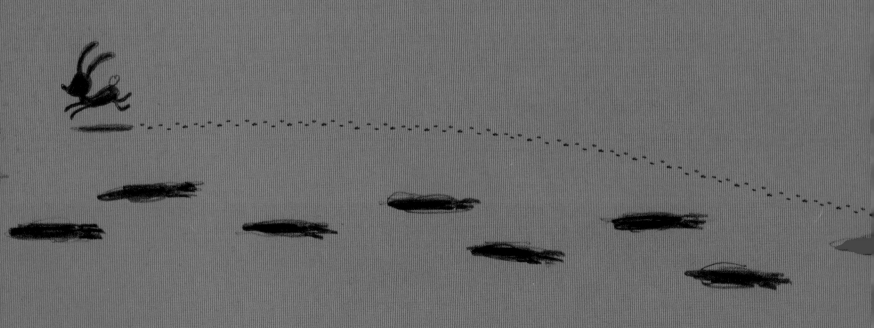

Do **YOU** ever
WONDER
if somewhere,

not too far away,

there *might* be . . .

MONSTERS?

Because just supposing there

are **monsters . . .**

. . . do you think that
this **monster**
might be licking his lips
and
thinking about . . .
YOU?

And if this monster *is*
thinking about you

maybe

he's thinking about you in an
EATING-YOU-UP
kind of way?

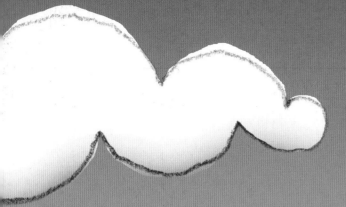

I hope not.

Because

he's coming to find you . . .

RIGHT NOW!

And as he bicycles bumpily
through a
dark and **terrible** forest

BUMP BUMPITY BUMP

do you think
he's **smiling** because
he remembered to pack
his **knife** and **fork**?

And as he crosses
the gloopy, schloopy swamp

GLOOP GLOOP SCHLOOP

do you think
he's imagining just

HOW GOOD

you'll taste
all covered in ketchup?

And as he tiptoes
through thorns and thistles

SCRITCH SCRATCH OUCH!
do you think
he'll decide that actually . . .

you'll taste *even* more **delicious**
squished and then **squashed** on to
HOT BUTTERED TOAST?

And at this very moment,
as he climbs into the cold and snowy mountains,
getting *closer*
and *closer*...
to **you**,
don't you think
he'll be feeling
VERY
HUNGRY
INDEED?

You're not **SCARED**, are you?

Because if he *is* feeling
very hungry indeed
while he searches high and low
and up and down
and in and out
all over town . . .

maybe you'll hear his **BIG** empty tummy

RRRRuUUuMMMmBLiNG
and
GGRRRRRuUUuMMMMmBLiNG?

And if you *do* hear a
RRRRUUUuMMMmBLlNG
and
GGRrrrRRuUUuMMMmbLlNG

you might *also* hear a
CREAK   CREAK   CREAK

as he starts to climb the stairs?

And as he opens your bedroom door

DO YOU THINK
   he's **licking his lips**
because he wants to
               gobble you up?

Oh no,
         it's MUCH worse than that!!!

THIS monster wants . . .

a disgustingly big

GOODNIGHT KISS!

KISSY

KISSY

KISSY!!

Because it's
bedtime for **monsters**
everywhere.

BIG ones like him . . .

and little ones,
just like **you.**

Did you *really* think he'd eat you up?

How silly!

Although

you *could* leave out

a little bedtime snack . . .

just in case.